# The Adventures of Larry the Lemur

# The Adventures of Larry the Lemur

*Ralph Castaneda*

iUniverse, Inc.
New York Lincoln Shanghai

## The Adventures of Larry the Lemur

iUniverse, Inc.

For information address:
iUniverse, Inc.
2021 Pine Lake Road, Suite 100
Lincoln, NE 68512
www.iuniverse.com

ISBN: 0-595-31815-0

Printed in the United States of America

# Contents

# The Beginning: The Legend of Larry the Lemur

The stories you are about to read concern a very special animal named Larry. What makes Larry special? Well, he talks, which is something that just about every animal cannot do. He also is highly intelligent and uses his brain to sometimes get into some very interesting situations. Situations that should not be attempted by real children.

For a more exhaustive and thorough look at real life Lemurs, one might set this book aside and find a nature book or ask a teacher for more information. If one would like to read some interesting stories about an enchanted Lemur who lives in an enchanted forest, then he or she would be highly encouraged to read on.

Here's a fact for those sticklers who are looking for at least one true fact: Lemurs in real life live on the Island of Madagascar.

# Chapter 1

## The Exterminator

Once upon a time there was a little Lemur named Larry. Of course, you probably figured that out from the title of our story. Little Larry was the middle child of a large family of Lemurs and as such was often overlooked. Unlike other Lemurs who would probably be upset at such a situation, Larry relished the freedom that he received from his insignificance. No one could keep him from his various explorations if they had forgotten that he even existed.

Larry's parents weren't neglectful or careless. They were just absentminded. When one has quite a large brood of Lemur children, one doesn't normally notice if one of them happens to wander off. It had been this way for most of the young Lemur's life. Larry took advantage of this situation to do things that other Lemurs only dreamed about.

This situation had made Larry quite resourceful and allowed him to come up with quick solutions to his problems. After all, one would have to be quite intelligent to learn how to change one's own diaper. He was often too impatient to wait for his parents to do it for him.

One of the most challenging events of Larry's young life occurred when he was still crawling around. On a visit to the house of his Lemur grandparents (there are a lot of things in the Lemur world that are described with the word *Lemur*) he had been mistakenly left behind. Normally, one would expect one's grandparents to simply take the child back home or place a call to one's parents reminding them of their forgetfulness. Unfortunately for Larry, his grandparents were quite hard of hearing and nearly blind.

A Lemur baby has numerous needs, much like a human one. Larry was no exception. You see, he had not yet learned how to change his own diaper and was quite hungry. He started crying, as many babies do when confronted with such a situation, but his grandparents could hear nary a peep. They were hard of hearing, remember. He also tried pulling at his grandmother's apron, but when she looked down, she could only see a blur. They were also quite blind, but of course, you already knew that too.

Larry's cries and pulls became even more desperate. What is a desperate pull like? That's something you would have known had you been there at the time. Apparently this desperation was paying off, as Larry's grandmother seemed to finally pay attention to him. "Carl," she said. Carl was the name of Larry's grandfather. "I believe that our home is now infested with rats. I feel them underfoot." The two grandparents wondered what to do and it was eventually decided to call a Lemur exterminator to take care of the problem.

Now what we mean by *Lemur exterminator* is not that he exterminated Lemurs. On the contrary, he was an exterminator who happened to be a Lemur. This is a very important distinction.

While the prospect of an exterminator arriving doesn't seem like it would be particularly helpful, it is worth noting that an exterminator would perhaps have better sight than two old Lemurs. Larry was quite positive that he could convince the exterminator that he was really a baby who needed care.

Soon enough, the exterminator showed up at the front door. Neatly decked out in a crisp exterminator's uniform and quite intelligent looking, Larry was very certain that he would soon find his needs met. "I am so pleased that you were able to get here so soon," said Larry's grandmother, "My husband and I are hard of both hearing and sight and it is quite distressing to have terrible rodents underfoot."

"Don't worry ma'am," reassured the exterminator, "I will do my best to help you with your problem." The exterminator smiled at Larry before embarking on a tour of the house. Larry's grandparents retreated to their kitchen to await the results of the tour when the exterminator returned to the living room with a puzzled look on his face. As all of us reading this already know, he had not found rodents of any kind. Actually, while it could be argued that Lemurs are a type of rodent, I doubt that they would share that feeling. In any case, the exterminator now stared at Larry as the excited baby Lemur did his best to act out his current situation. Not being able to speak yet, he cleverly let the exterminator know that he needed to be attended to. He also threw in a request to be reunited with his parents as well.

Strangely enough, this precise performance of Larry's current predicament produced an odd reaction. The exterminator ran out of the house and returned with a book labeled *Rat Psychology*. Obviously, Larry could not read yet, so he knew nothing of the book's contents. For all Larry knew, the book was titled *Infant*

*Care* and outlined the proper steps for changing a diaper. Actually, this was precisely what Larry suspected. His suspicions were obviously incorrect, but Larry didn't guess this until he heard what the exterminator had to say next.

"I believe that this little rat must believe that he is a baby. Quite fascinating," the exterminator murmured to himself. At this point, it might be a good idea to bring to mind those times when you go from the happiest of heights to the saddest of lows. That was what it felt like for Larry once he realized that this exterminator was not going to help him. In fact, things were now quite worse because the exterminator would probably try to exterminate Larry.

Larry thought about his predicament. Why would the exterminator believe that a baby Lemur was really a rat? Obviously the exterminator must believe every thing he is told. Of course, one knows that this is quite ridiculous. While one must believe most things that one is told, especially if there is no evidence to the contrary, it is not a good idea to believe something when direct evidence exists to the contrary. For example, if a clerk were to say that all of the merchandise was out on display, one would have to believe it to be true. It would be rude to walk to the storage area of the store to check. Not to mention how dangerous it might be. Besides, the storage areas in the back of stores are quite small and probably not big enough to keep merchandise stored for very long. However, if the same clerk were to say that an item was not in stock when it was actually in plain sight, a reasonable person would believe his or her eyes and not what he or she was told. Unfortunately, our discussion of store clerks and store backrooms was doing little to help Larry. The rather dense exterminator was more willing to believe a nearly blind woman over his very own eyes and this was causing much distress on the part of Larry. How could he prove that he was really a baby Lemur and not a rat?

At this time, the exterminator was still engrossed in his book, oohing and aahing at various points. Larry then remembered that rats do not speak, at least in any language recognizable to man or Lemur. So he thought that he could convince the exterminator and his grandmother of his Lemurness if he could just concentrate and say something, but what? How could he do it?

Larry tried to think of something that could grab their attention before it was too late. Even if he could think of something to say, how could he do it? He wasn't sure that he was capable of speech yet—much like a rat. Since rats never, ever speak, they would have to assume that he was a Lemur. Larry knew that he would eventually be able to speak, but would he be able to do it in time? Just then his grandmother came into the room.

"Have you rid our house of the filthy vermin yet?" she queried. The exterminator looked up from his reading.

"Not yet, ma'am, I see the main culprit right here and I believe that he may think that he is a baby." Larry now knew that the time was right. He mustered up all of his vocal strength and said a word that he had heard one of his siblings say earlier, a word that had gotten a huge reaction from his grandmother.

"Grandma!" There—Larry had said it. Or had he? He wouldn't know if he'd said it correctly until he'd seen his grandmother's reaction.

"Little Larry? What are you still doing here? Your parents must have left you." She had finally noticed Larry and picked him up. "Oh, you could use a new diaper too. I hope that those rats didn't get you." The exterminator looked confused. "This is your grandchild?"

"Yes. His parents must have left him. Now about that rat…"

"He's, uh, gone," replied the exterminator, and not too untruthfully too. Since Larry was obviously not a rat, the *vermin* of which Larry's grandmother spoke was now *gone*.

"How much do we owe you, kind sir?" asked Larry's grandmother. The exterminator thought for a second.

"Nothing, ma'am. Consider it a gift."

"Thank you so much!" she shouted. He tipped his hat and walked out to his van. Larry was promptly changed and he soon found himself back home with his absent-minded parents.

Despite everything, what did they all learn from this? Larry's parents thought they had learned never to forget their children down someone's house, but they actually learned nothing in that regard. The exterminator learned not to always believe what he is told, a lesson that has been of great use to him. You won't find out how though, because these stories are not about an exterminator who happens to be a Lemur. What did Larry learn you ask? Well, Larry learned a valuable lesson, which will be of extreme importance later on in his life, that he can use his intelligence to get out of danger.

It would be wonderful to write that they all lived happily ever after and end the story here, but that would not prove to be the case. People who live "happily ever after" at the end of a story probably never do another thing in their lives that would be interesting to the story reading public. Fortunately for us, Larry does have even more stories and adventures that make quite entertaining reading.

# Chapter 2

## The Jumping Machine

As you probably know already from reading the previous story, Larry the Lemur is quite an intelligent child who often finds himself in some very interesting situations. At least, they are situations that are interesting to us. Perhaps Larry thinks of them more as being challenging than interesting.

Anyhow, all that is beside the point, for now we find Larry literally up a tree. However, since the story of how Larry got there is quite interesting, we shall leave him there for a moment to look back at how he got into this predicament.

Little Larry has grown much since we left him in the last story. Now he is a full-fledged toddler, toddling about and getting into mischief. Larry rarely means to get into trouble, but like many children, he really can't help it when his best intentions go awry. He didn't mean for his last experiment to end with a small kitchen fire, but that doesn't mean that it didn't happen all the same. He also didn't plan for his father to lose his hair by drinking one of Larry's potions, but that didn't stop his father from going bald either.

This time, Larry was supposed to be playing in his family's large backyard with his siblings, but he soon became quite bored and wandered out past the yard's boundaries. Of course, nobody noticed this because of the large amount of siblings Larry had. Perhaps if you were in charge of such a large group of children, you would be vigilant and make sure that nobody wandered off. Fortunately for Larry, his parents were quite absentminded and they noticed nothing.

As Larry hiked off, he noticed the world around him. He loved these hikes because they allowed him to see things that he had never seen and think thoughts that he had never thought before. It was during these walks that Larry got many of his greatest ideas. Well, at least, Larry thought that they were great. His father and the Lemur Firefighters who battled the kitchen fire would probably disagree.

This wandering was no exception. Instantly, ideas flew into his head. Many of the ideas were large and impractical. A few of them were extremely possible, thought Larry. Wouldn't his siblings adore him if he used some common ingredients to put together a fireworks display? In fact, Larry was thinking about how old he would have to be before he would ever be allowed to handle fire without his parents being upset, when his eyes happened upon a grasshopper. Larry then began thinking about how wondrous it would be to have the ability to jump about as one pleased. Luckily, the thought of mixing fireworks had quickly disappeared from his head. To this day the Lemur firefighters have no idea how much they should thank that grasshopper.

Anyway, Larry began looking at the objects around him to see if he could construct any sort of jumping device with them. Soon, Larry had constructed a makeshift device that looked like it would work as a jumping machine. "This is great," said Larry to no one in particular, "I think that I shall call it a Jumpometer!" Of course, this is a rather ridiculous name, since one would assume that a device that ended with *ometer* would be an item that measured something. Larry's crude invention measured nothing. However, since Larry invented the device, it is not really up to us to judge the name he gave it.

While we were arguing the merits of the device's chosen name, Larry was readying a plan to test his new device. He looked around to find a flat, level, relatively treeless area where he could test things out. While the device wouldn't necessarily need a flat, level, relatively treeless area in which to operate, Larry was thinking about his own safety.

By this time, his invention had attracted quite a few birds that closely watched as Larry readied his contraption. Since the birds were not making noise, Larry let them watch. Also, since Larry relished attention, he secretly thought how grand it was to have an appreciative audience. Had he invented a mind reading device, Larry would have known that his quiet audience was more of a scornful one than one that was appreciative, but at least they were paying attention to him.

Unable to find a suitable location nearby, Larry tried to pick up his invention and carry it to a better spot. Unfortunately, this invention was quite heavy for a little Lemur of Larry's stature to carry. Larry knew that this wasn't the best place for the test to occur, but he also didn't want to wait until he grew into a Lemur teen to test out the invention either.

So, Larry decided to take his chances and began calculating a way to bounce that would fling him into the air away from the trees. After about half an hour of coming up with calculations that would only make sense to him, Larry came upon a plan that he was sure would not get him into any trouble. Of course, Larry always thought that his plans would not cause too much trouble. His plan is much too complex to go into here, but as you've no doubt figured out by the beginning of the story, Larry ended up stuck in a tree. Not just any tree, mind you, but the tree that those scornful birds were nesting in.

Larry looked around dazed. Since the sensation caused by the jump had made him woozy, he had lost track of himself for a minute. Now that his eyes and mind were getting used to things, he realized that he was stuck in the tree surrounded by the birds that had once served as his audience from above. They looked at him curiously. None of them had ever seen a lemur this closely before, since they spent most of their spare time high above them. One of the more inquisitive birds approached Larry and gently began poking him with the tip of his beak.

"Ouch! Stop that!" shouted Larry, clearly upset not only with the birds but also with himself for getting stuck in the tree. The birds gasped.

"That creature can talk!" shouted one of the birds. This enraged Larry further because he hated it when anyone assumed that he didn't know how to talk. He then made the mistake of trying to swat the birds away. This then enraged the birds. And trust me, enraged grown up birds with sharp beaks are definitely scarier than a small lemur toddler.

In his desperate attempt to flee the pecking birds, Larry moved deeper and deeper into the tree becoming ever more lost. Also, Larry had completely forgotten that he was terribly afraid of heights. In fact, all the excitement of coming up with a new invention had made Larry forget about his fears. Why a

Lemur suffering from vertigo would even attempt to create a jumping machine is a question best left unanswered.

We now find Larry stuck where he was at the beginning of our story. The birds had long since stopped trying to annoy him, so at least he no longer had to worry about getting pecked. It seems that the audience of birds was merely resting on a long flight to their yearly vacations, but since this book isn't titled *Bird Vacation Spots* it must be left to our imaginations where they were heading and what they did once they got there.

Of course, none of these discussions would have been of interest to Larry since he was desperately trying to figure out a way down that wouldn't make him even more frightened than he already was. Every time that he tried to climb down the tree, his extreme fear of heights frightened him back onto the branch he was stuck on. He even tried closing his eyes and climbing down, but that obviously didn't help him out much. You see, since he wasn't familiar with this particular tree he kept imagining himself falling all the way down because he didn't step on a branch correctly.

Suddenly, a rather strong looking bird flew up to Larry, who was cowering in the tree and examined him carefully. Since he was crying with his face down in his lap, he didn't notice her until she tried to comfort him with her wing. "There, there young mouse, everything will be okay. Maybe this will teach you not to try to eat the eggs out of a bird's nest."

Of course, there were numerous things wrong with that statement and Larry turned from sad to angry rather quickly. "I'm not a mouse! And I don't eat bird's eggs! I jumped up here and now I'm stuck!" The bird looked at him curiously.

"Really? I could have sworn you looked like a mouse. And when I lay my eggs, I have to watch out because the mice like to come and steal them." She paused, "Wait a second. You're not trying to trick me, are you? Perhaps you want me to take you into my confidence so that I'll invite you to my nest for dinner. Then, when my back is turned you'll make a quick dinner out of my eggs. Is that your game?" Larry thought it was quite ludicrous that the bird thought that he would even consider such a plan when there were so many better ways to get the eggs that would be a lot easier to do. While Larry contemplated these other ideas, the bird grew impatient and suspicious. "You're trying to come up with a lie to draw attention away from your potential egg thievery, aren't you?" Larry woke up from his thoughts and quickly realized that he could use this bird to get out of the tree.

"No! I'm telling you, I don't eat eggs. My problem is that I need to get out of this tree. You look strong enough. Maybe you could lift me out of here?"

"And where will I lift you young man, to my nest perhaps?"

"Yes. I mean, no. Carry me to the ground. I just want to get back on solid ground so that I can go home." The bird looked at him carefully.

"Hmm, this could be part of your plan. I carry you down, and then you invite me over to your place for dinner. Of course, I'll be obliged to invite you to my nest in turn and then you'll surely gobble my eggs. No thank you, young man." She then began to fly out of the tree.

"Wait! I promise! I won't invite you to my house to get your confidence and I won't eat your eggs."

"Why young man," the bird began, "that is just plain rude!" Larry was puzzled.

"Rude? To not eat your eggs?"

"No, young man. To not invite me over to your place as a reward for getting you out of the tree."

"But you said you thought it was a ruse to get me in so that I can eat your eggs. So I promise I won't invite you."

"Young man, that's not good manners. You should always reward someone when they extend a kindness to you, even if it does seem suspicious to do so." Larry thought for a few seconds and came up with an idea.

"What if I give you my newest invention? It's a Jumpometer!" The bird looked at him curiously.

"A Jumpometer? You mean a device that measures jumping? That doesn't sound like it would be of interest to me. I rarely jump over anything."

"No, it's a device that makes you jump higher and faster than you could on your own. And besides, if I gave it to you, then I wouldn't have to invite you over to my house and you wouldn't have to return the favor..." Larry quickly ran out of breath and was relieved to see the bird nodding which meant that he probably didn't have to continue.

"I see. So even if I don't need to measure my jumping, then we're even." Larry was annoyed that the bird was still making the wrong assumption about what his invention did but was happy nonetheless since it looked like she was going to get him down. Carefully, she rubbed her feet together. "Hang on, young mouse."

"I'm not a..." Larry began before being scooped up by the bird. His fear of heights got the best of him for a second but he quite enjoyed the view and was soon out of the tree and set beside the so-called Jumpometer. The bird looked at it carefully.

"Why this doesn't measure jumping," noted the bird, "It's a jumping machine! This will be useful for teaching my birds how to fly. How will I ever thank you? Perhaps a gift box of some sort?"

"Well, you did get me out of the tree," Larry reminded her.

"Yes, but...Okay, I'll pick out something nice then. Do mice still like cheese?" This question angered Larry even more because he definitely wasn't a mouse, but he merely nodded his head and took his leave.

He glanced back for a second and was happy to see the bird trying the invention out. Since most adults didn't seem to like his inventions, he got a great sense of pride that one of them was appreciated, but he thought better of sharing this with his family. They wouldn't understand since he wasn't supposed to be playing outside of the yard anyway.

As usual, no one had noticed that he was missing when he rejoined his siblings in the Lemur backyard. And, while his parents were very surprised when a large bird presented them with a special gift basket of cheeses for Larry one evening not long after, they didn't question it. After all, if you had a large family of hungry Lemurs to feed, you wouldn't question a gift of free food would you?

# Chapter 3

## The Thinking Tree

As always, there was much activity going on in Larry the Lemur's house. Larry's mother was quite frantic as the daily rigors of running a household filled with young Lemurs wore on. There was a lot of cooking to be done, chores, seeing after the younger ones. It was quite easy to not miss one particular Lemur. After all, Larry did not challenge authority like his older siblings or need changings and constant feedings like the younger Lemurs. It is on this day that we join Larry on one of his wanderings.

Larry had snuck off quite early. He was intent on finding a new thinking tree after his old one fell victim to one of his experiments that was inspired by a long day of thinking. It could be said that the inspiration provided by the tree led to its own demise. The task of finding a new tree would seem to be an easy one—there were hundreds around the woods that Larry called home. Also, being of short stature, one would assume that most trees would look the same to Larry. Larry, however, was looking for something quite special, and he was sure that he could find it if he walked around long enough.

He looked at tree after tree and came up with many excuses for not choosing a particular one—not enough leaves, too close to home, not conducive to thinking, etc. He soon came upon a tree that by all appearances was perfect. Larry knew that he could do some great thinking there. As he began making himself at home, he heard a piercing screech. He looked up to notice that a hostile looking owl had taken a spot on a branch not far from where Larry was standing. What does a hostile owl look like? Perhaps not much different from what we would expect an owl to look like normally, but to a fellow animal he looked quite peeved.

"What are you doing young lemur?" queried the owl. "I hope that you aren't thinking of making this your home."

Larry was shocked. "No, I don't want to live here. I'm just look-ing for a new thinking tree. You see my old tree—"

"Young lady, I'm not interested in hearing about your tree problems. I just want to make it clear that this tree is quite clearly where I come to roost." This statement angered Larry quite a bit, as it would any boy, human or Lemur.

"I'm not a young lady. I'm a boy Lemur. And I just want to use this tree to sit under while I compose my thoughts."

"Yes, it will start out that way. Then soon you will bring other Lemurs all of which will be quite noisy and upsetting. No, I'm afraid that you will have to find some other place to do your thinking."

Larry was flabbergasted. None of the birds who roosted in his old tree seemed to care that he used it to think under. Of course, they did care very much when his experiment went awry and the tree fell over. Up until then, however, they were quite willing to share. Larry then thought about—

"Don't just stand there staring, young Lemur. Move on now," the owl interrupted while Larry was thinking the last paragraph, "I have some thinking of my own to do."

"Wait a minute," said Larry, "I thought that owls stayed asleep during the day and woke up only during the night. I believe that I read that somewhere. What are you doing awake?"

This seemed to annoy the owl even further. "Such insolence from you young Lemurs these days! It isn't up to me to explain myself to you. Besides, you shouldn't believe everything you read. I certainly don't!"

Larry decided that he was better off finding a different tree somewhere else. It obviously wouldn't be a good idea to stay here with a screeching owl causing problems. It simply wasn't good for thinking. Larry left the tree and quickly chose one nearby. Not because it was perfect, but because it would give him a close up view of his new enemy, the owl.

Suddenly, Larry heard a loud noise and looked up at a loud cawing buzzard. The buzzard kept dive-bombing Larry, all the while cawing up a storm. "Caw! Caw! Caw!" went the buzzard. Larry tried to shoo the bird away to no avail. One might wonder why the bird didn't simply tell Larry to go away. Well, if one were a human, that is, one would wonder such a thing. As every animal knows, buzzards, like rats, do not speak any decipherable language whatsoever.

Dejected, Larry gave up and wandered off in search of yet another thinking tree. If it had been this hard to find one before, maybe he wouldn't have even bothered to have one. Also, a flock of birds would still have a fully functioning tree, rather than a toppled over stump.

Finally, Larry found another perfect thinking tree that was not populated by any birds, annoying or otherwise. Larry marked his map and made himself at home. The tree had a perfect hiding place, big enough to hide a treasure trove of items.

Larry then laid back and began a productive afternoon of thinking. Unfortunately, he wasted most of his thinking time coming up with ways to get revenge on a pompous owl and an annoying buzzard. Since most of his ideas were not even remotely possible, and perhaps even illegal, he went back to his house without having had a productive thought. He appeared completely distracted at dinner, but since his parents had so many children to look after they didn't even notice.

The very next day, Larry snuck off to his new thinking tree and struggled yet again. It seemed that no matter how hard he tried, he couldn't come up with even one good idea. This predicament led Larry to believe that maybe this tree was not conducive to thinking. Perhaps he needed to stand his ground and force that crummy old owl to share that tree, he thought. How could he do that? Especially since he hadn't had one good thought since choosing this tree?

Larry grudgingly tromped home, not having come up with any new ideas yet again. The stress of this weighed on him heavily and he struggled to fall asleep that night. The owl even appeared in his dreams. At least, he thought it was the same owl that had been giving him such a big headache. A second glance from his dream self had revealed the owl to be one that he had known previously. A rather large cat soon appeared and frightened the owl away.

Suddenly, Larry awoke and shouted, "That's it!" He had apparently come up with a plan to rid himself of that pesky owl.

He had also awakened half of his siblings who shared the same room. A few of the younger ones began crying and Larry's extremely tired parents raced in to see what the problem was.

They caught Larry sitting straight up and very much awake. His father grabbed one of the children and told Larry: "Larry, did you have another of your dreams? I sure hope you're not planning some sort of invention!" Larry's face turned bright red.

"No, dad. I promise," Larry somewhat fibbed. You see, while he did have an idea to get rid of that miserable owl, it didn't involve an invention. Fortunately, Larry's father didn't even hear his response since he was busying himself with calming down the awakened Lemur children. Larry tried to go back to sleep, but the noise that his brothers and sisters were making, coupled with the excitement of having a plan kept him awake.

The very next morning, Larry put his plan into action. He carefully made his way to the living room and looked at one of the rugs on the floor. It wasn't exactly what he was looking for, but he figured that it would do. Perhaps, thought Larry, the owl would be so tired from his all night foraging that he wouldn't actually notice anything wrong.

Larry snuck outside quickly with the rug and hid in a bush that was just out of the line of sight of the owl, which was apparently sleeping. Wrapping himself in the rug, Larry crawled over to the tree and began meowing. You see, Larry was hoping to pass for a cat, since he assumed that all owls were afraid of them. This owl, however, was in such a deep sleep that he merely ruffled his feathers and continued sleeping. Larry stepped up his meowing and also tried to pretend he was climbing up the tree.

Finally, the owl opened one eye and looked down at Larry. "Hmm, it's you again. I thought I had asked you to not hang out here. Is that a rug you're wearing?" asked the owl. Larry was deeply upset and took off his costume.

"How did you know it was me and not a cat?" asked Larry. The owl grinned.

"Well, young man, cats don't have a checkerboard pattern on their fur. Besides, what was the idea behind dressing like a cat?"

"Aren't owls afraid of cats?"

The owl began laughing. "No, I don't believe owls are afraid of cats in general, but I do have a cousin who was afraid of cats. His name is—"

"Hawthorne?" asked Larry. He was hoping that perhaps this owl was related to his old friend.

"Why yes, it is. Do you know him?"

"Yes. He used to live in one of my old thinking trees, one that fell—heh." Larry was afraid that he had let the cat out of the bag, so to speak.

"Wow, what a small forest. Why, you're practically family! I'll tell you what. Why don't we compromise? You can use this tree to think under as long as you stay quiet." Larry almost jumped for joy.

"Really? That would be great! Thank you!"

"One thing that I've been wondering, though. Why do you need a tree to think under?"

"Well, I've been trying to think under one of the trees over there, but haven't had any luck."

"That's it? Well, you sure thought up this scheme, didn't you? It was quite clever, actually. You should be proud of yourself."

"You're right! Maybe I don't need a tree after all. Actually—" Larry cut himself off when he realized that the owl had fallen back asleep. Deciding to leave well enough alone, Larry quietly began reading the book he had brought with him.

Perhaps, Larry thought, he didn't need a tree to think under after all. He then remembered that he had just dragged his mother's best rug through the dirt and needed to get it back to the living room fully cleaned before she noticed it was missing. "This might take awhile," Larry said to himself, so he sat back against the tree and tried to think of a plan.

# Chapter 4

## A Day at Lemurland

Today was the day that Larry and his siblings had been waiting for—the day of the family trip to Lemurland. As you've probably guessed, Lemurland is the biggest and best amusement park in the Lemur world. From the moment a young Lemur is born, he or she instantly desires to make a trek to Lemurland and Larry was no different.

As you've heard on at least three other occasions, Larry has quite a few siblings. It would certainly seem to be quite an impossible task to undertake a trip to a large theme park with such a large group of children. Larry's grandparents, however, were so insistent that everyone visit the park that they not only volunteered to pay for it, but to also tag along and watch some of the children. A saner person, or Lemur, would have just given Larry's parents wads of cash to visit the park and left them to figure out the logistics of taking such a large group of children there, but his grandparents actually relished the challenge.

So, let's imagine this Lemur family just inside the gates at Lemurland. All those Lemur children with only two absent minded parents and two nearly deaf and blind grandparents to corral them. It was quite a scene as Larry's elder family members tried to divide the children up into groups and then split up to see the Lemurland sights in smaller, easier to manage groups.

Of course, in the most predictable of occurrences, Larry split off from his assigned group to try to explore Lemurland on his own. He actually got quite far into the park before he realized that one of his younger Lemur siblings was following him around.

Larry was quite surprised to see little...well, he wasn't quite sure which one of his siblings this little tyke actually was. Of course, Larry had definitely seen him before, but with all of the thinking and inventions and planning Larry had not really committed the names of his brothers and sisters to memory. So he stared carefully at his brother, trying to remember his name. Larry's thinking ended when his brother spoke out with an urgent request. Some might have argued that it was more of a demand.

Larry's brother pointed in no particular direction and shouted "Wide!" Larry was puzzled.

"Wide?" he asked. "Are you pondering the width of the walkways here at Lemurland?"

Larry's brother shook his head and sighed. "Wide!"

"Oh, you probably want to ride something." This bothered Larry, because he had planned on using this opportunity to wander around Lemurland and come up with some new ideas for inventions. He didn't plan on escorting any of his siblings around on rides. Larry's brother fidgeted while he thought of what to do. Soon, Larry had no choice, as his brother merely grabbed his hand and pulled him in the direction of the nearest *wide*.

Larry looked up at the sign and noticed that he was being dragged to a ride called *Happy Lemurs*. He wasn't sure what the ride was even about, but the decorative mural out front showed various smiling Lemurs engaged in different activities. Before Larry knew it, he and his brother were strapped into a colorful ride vehicle and whisked into the world of the *Happy Lemurs* which was a frightening collection of robotic Lemurs happily singing along to the insipid music that played over the loud-speakers. Larry looked over at his brother who was beaming from the experience and swaying to the beat.

In an effort to make the most of a bad situation, Larry carefully inspected the ride vehicle and the track to uncover the secrets behind its design. Just as Larry was about to get an idea for an elaborate transit system that he could employ inside the Lemur house, his brother tapped him on the shoulder and pointed at the dancing robots. "Look, wide!" he shouted, as if to chastise Larry for daring to look elsewhere. Lucky for Larry's parents, he totally forgot about building any sort of transit system featuring motorized vehicles through their house. And if you have to ask why they were lucky, just imagine what you would think if your house was very nearly destroyed…

Not soon enough, the ride was complete and Larry found himself standing outside with his brother who was frantically looking around for another *wide*. In fact, since Larry still could not remember his brother's name, he had settled on simply calling him *Wide*. Soon enough, *Wide's* eyes were drawn to a hokey looking boat ride that apparently went through miniature re-creations of great moments in Lemur history. Despite not really wanting to go on any of the rides at Lemurland, Larry was quite eager to get on this one once he realized what it was about.

The brothers were again strapped in and were now embarking on a journey through Lemur history. *Wide* looked in wonder at the moving robots as they re-enacted historic moments. Larry smiled and figured that his brother probably didn't understand or appreciate the ride as he did. The ride featured numerous Lemurs inventing machines, discovering new places and doing the sort of things that Larry had always dreamed of. He soon found himself imagining how Lemurland would honor his achievements in the ride once he became famous. Just as he got around to picturing how his robot self would look, he felt a tug on his shirt. The ride was over and his brother was eager to run off to the next ride.

Suddenly, a great rush of Lemurs began scrambling out of a theater where presumably a show of some sort had just ended. Larry stared at the marquee and noticed that it was a show featuring realistic robotic Lemur figures. Excited at the prospect of seeing a show featuring such elaborate inventions, Larry rushed in, quite forgetting that he was navigating the park with his younger brother. Soon enough, the show had ended and it had inspired Larry to run home immediately and invent some sort of robot.

At this time, Larry finally remembered his brother. He frantically looked everywhere and came to the conclusion that little *Wide* had gone missing—a conclusion that we had previously come to in the last paragraph, as you no doubt remember. Larry's first thought was to rush to the Lemur Relations office at Lemurland and ask for their help in searching for *Wide*. Of course, he then realized that not only did he not remember what his brother was wearing, a helpful bit of information to have if you're looking for a lost person or Lemur, but he had also forgotten his name. Certainly, you remember that Larry only called him *Wide* because of the littler Lemur's mispronunciation of the word *ride*.

Larry's second thought was to find his parents and get their help, but he was afraid of what they would say if they knew that he had run off and lost one of their children. When you are in trouble, you should definitely seek the help of your parents or a security guard. Definitely, if you were to wander into Lemurland and find yourself lost, you should head towards the front gate and find the Lemur Relations office. The friendly Lemurs there will not only help you find your parents, but they would also entertain you with a coloring book or two. Larry, on the other hand, was doing the exact opposite of what he should have done. An impulsive Lemur like Larry doesn't always do the right thing, but then if he did, this book would be quite boring and you'd probably be reading something else.

While we debated the merits of finding help when one is lost, Larry was still trying to figure out what to do. While we have just concluded what a smart and responsible child should do when faced with this dilemma, Larry was thinking of a way out of his problem without having to do what we just discussed. Unfortunately, his solution was really just to walk around in circles and hope that his little brother would just appear magically out of thin air. Since even in the Lemur world, this type of event rarely occurred, Larry's plan was definitely not working.

Suddenly, a thought began to appear in Larry's head as part of a desperate attempt to fix this problem without having to bring in the proper authorities. Larry remembered that coming from a large brood of Lemurs had made mealtimes an adventure. He and the rest of his siblings had grown accustomed to having spirited competitions for things like *seconds* and, when his parents were at their most forgetful, even *firsts*. Don't worry, they always had plenty for everyone, it just meant that sometimes a little Lemur might have to wait a little while longer for dinner.

Anyhow, Larry was almost certain that little *Wide* was partial to popcorn. Whenever Larry had come upon some popcorn of his own, *Wide* was right there, ready to take a few handfuls. It was almost as if he had a sixth sense for that type of thing. For a quick second, Larry wondered if he could find a place in the park where he might be able to purchase some popcorn.

Fortunately for him, the folks at Lemurland had apparently thought of everything. In an attempt to maximize their profits, they had seen fit to place a food cart of some sort every few feet along every walkway. About the only thing that Larry had to worry about was finding the correct food stand.

Soon enough, Larry made his way to the correct cart and fished out the correct amount of money. The line moved quickly and soon enough, Larry found himself at the front of it. He made an elaborate show of handing the money to the worker and accepting the popcorn in return. Then he looked for a bench and theatrically began eating his popcorn. "I am lucky," Larry said to himself rather loudly, "I get to eat all of this popcorn by myself!"

Larry took a quick glimpse around. Other than scaring off some of the Lemurs who chose not to sit near a ranting young man, he had accomplished nothing. *Wide* was nowhere to be found. Larry sighed and pondered his parents' reaction to all of this. Perhaps they would pay more attention to his every move, something that would sound great to some children, but would most certainly end Larry's great adventures, a possibility that made Larry quite sad.

Suddenly, Larry saw a tiny lemur hand reaching into his pop-corn box. His first response to this action, coming from a big family was to slap the hand away. Larry, however, remembered that he should actually be happy, since this meant that he had found his brother. Little *Wide* sat with a huge smile on his face and made quick work of eating the popcorn.

Larry, meanwhile, wondered what his little brother might say to his parents. Perhaps he would tell them everything and Larry would have to suffer under his parents' watch for the rest of his younger days. Gone would be his alone time, his thinking tree time, his wondrous inventions!

As little *Wide* wiped his mouth, Larry wondered what the first words would be from his mouth. Would he blackmail Larry? Accuse him of being a terrible brother? Larry needn't worry. The first, and only, word out of his brother's mouth was, of course, "Wide!" And *wide* they did. Larry even braved another trip through the world of the so-called *Happy Lemurs*.

At the end of the day, Larry and little *Wide* re-introduced themselves into the family, having spent a marvelous day together. Larry even started to feel guilty about not having remembered the name of his brother. As his father went through the customary roll call of the Lemur children, Larry wracked his brain to figure out what his brother's name was before their father got to them. His father would be reading little *Wide*'s name off of the list any minute now, but Larry wanted to think of it before his father said it out loud. Was his name Ben? Bob? Abe? Sammy? Maybe it was Jose? None of those seemed right to Larry as his father quickly approached.

Just then, it became obvious to Larry just what his brother's name was. Excited at his remembrance, Larry blurted it out just as his father was about to. "Of course! Rider!" Larry's dad smiled.

"Yes, and last but not least, our beloved Larry," said Larry's father as he patted both Larry and Rider on their heads. Larry could have kicked himself when he realized that his brother's name was right in front of him the whole time. Larry's guilt about not remembering Rider's name disappeared when Rider gave him a big hug before they left the park. Either his brother didn't realize Larry's memory lapse, or more importantly, he didn't care.

# Chapter 5

## Larry and the Turtle

As we've seen so far, Larry can be quite curious about the world around him. This can be a wondrous thing when one takes into account the feelings and thoughts of those around him or her. Unfortunately, when Larry gets his mind set on something, he doesn't always think of the problems that his actions might cause.

For many of the animals living in Larry's forest, this oversight on his part can prove calamitous. Remember those poor animals that had ended up homeless because he toppled over their tree? Unfortunately for them, they had no prior warning of Larry's plans. They just came home to their tree at the end of the day and found it had fallen over and was pretty much useless.

Such was the predicament of the many animals that had fallen victim to Larry's so-called experiments. Until he met a plucky turtle named Elliot, that is. You see, Larry's experiment required—actually, it would probably be best to start at the very beginning of that fateful day.

Larry had gone to his latest thinking tree and began sketching things in his notebook. One of the pictures that he found himself sketching was of a turtle, but something didn't seem right. At least it didn't seem right to Larry. Since many of us have accepted the fact that turtles exist and that they look a certain way, we wouldn't look at a picture of one and think it was wrong, but Larry's mind certainly works differently from those of nearly everyone else, so he puzzled over this particular sketch.

So what exactly made Larry take a second look at the picture of the turtle? It was the odd shape of a turtle's shell. He simply couldn't figure out if a turtle could, if flipped on its back, recover and right itself.

He thought of several different ways that he could test this out, but couldn't think of one that he felt would perfectly answer his question. He then remembered that he actually knew a turtle named Elliot. Maybe, he thought, Elliot would be willing to help him out in his experiment.

So, Larry ran over to Elliot's house to find out if his friend was willing to help. Unfortunately for Larry, Elliot was nowhere to be found. Larry did find Elliot's tiny twin sisters Lexi and Monique. Figuring that they might know where their brother was, he decided to ask them just that question.

The twins, on the other hand, didn't want to be very helpful. Rather than answer Larry's question, they merely kept staring at each other and giggling uncontrollably. This annoyed Larry very much.

"What's so funny?" he asked, "I just asked a question." The girls looked at each other again and laughed.

"We're twins, Larry," noted Lexi, "We don't have to use our mouths to speak to each other. We can…"

"Read each other's minds!" finished Monique. The two giggled again.

Perhaps at this point, it might be useful to ponder the truthfulness of their statement. Were the twins actually able to read each other's minds? Some people believe that twins have a very special bond that would make mind reading possible. Others think that twins just make things up like that to confuse those of us who have no twins. In any case, finding out if twins possess any sort of mind reading powers would be an exciting and worthwhile experiment, if only to prove a pair of excitable and giggly twin turtles wrong. Unfortunately, Larry's mind still centered on his upside down turtle experiment and he completely missed the opportunity to make an even bigger discovery.

Larry, meanwhile, was quite impatient with Lexi and Monique's giggling and eager to find his friend. "Okay. If you see your brother, could you tell him I was here and was looking for him?" Larry thought that was a reasonable request, but it only resulted in more giggling from the turtle duo. "Well...?"

"Oh, we heard you Larry," replied Monique, "and my sister and I agree that we will pass on your message." The two giggled some more. Larry cautiously thanked them for their help and backed away.

Since Larry wasn't completely sure if his message would get to Elliot, he began his own search of the forest. Larry looked in all the places that he would have expected a turtle to hang out in and eventually found his friend. One might have expected to read about the different locations in which Larry looked for his friend, but since this book is not entitled *Turtle Hangouts*, those places are best left to the imagination of the reader.

In any case, Larry was quite surprised to find his buddy just hanging out lazily by a small brook. "Hey there, Elliot! What are you doing around here?" asked Larry. The small turtle looked up at Larry and smiled.

Actually, being a turtle, Elliot had to look up at just about everyone.

"If you had twin sisters, you'd probably understand," answered Elliot, "so, what's up?" Larry's first instinct was to challenge Elliot's statement. After all, having a large group of Lemur siblings was no easy task. However, Larry was eager to get his experiment started so he ignored the statement.

"Well, I had this idea..."

"Stop for a second, Larry. This isn't one of your regular ideas, is it? Remember when you toppled that tree? I almost got crushed that day." Larry gulped. This was probably going to be harder than he thought, since his idea was quite risky.

"Well," began Larry.

"Oh no. I know that tone. I'm not getting hooked into one of your experiments again."

"But we're best friends," protested Larry.

"Best friends or not, I'm not getting into trouble again. What is this crazy experiment anyway?"

"Well, I don't see how we could possibly get into trouble, since this experiment doesn't really involve anyone else. You see, I was wondering if turtles can right themselves if they've fallen on their backs."

"Oh, no!" protested Elliot. "I'm not putting myself at risk for one of your strange thoughts. Besides, I believe that we can right ourselves after we've fallen on our backs, so there goes your little experiment."

"But Elliot, are you sure that you could right yourself? Have you ever seen a turtle that actually did that after falling on his back?"

"No, I have luckily never been around a poor turtle who had fallen on his back, nor do I know anyone who has. I just figure that it could be done."

"Yeah, but you don't know that for sure. Wouldn't you rather be sure?"

"Well, I don't know for sure if I'd survive a fall from a high tree, but I don't think it would be a good idea to try it. Hmm. I have to get back home. I'll see you later, Larry." With that rejection, Elliot turned and made his slow but steady way back to his house.

Larry was devastated since it didn't appear that he would ever get the answer he was searching for. Just that second, however, he realized something that we had previously mentioned—the fact that most of the subjects of his previous experiments were quite unaware that they were actually participating in an experiment. Larry realized that he too had to head home, but he promised himself that he would go to his thinking tree as soon as possible in the morning to figure out a way to have his experiment without Elliot knowing about it.

The next morning, Larry made his way to the thinking tree and spent the entire morning trying to think of a way to rope Elliot into his experiment without him knowing. The obvious ideas came to mind—running up to Elliot and flipping him over, hiring someone else to run up to Elliot and flip him over, etc. Larry, however, enjoyed his friendship with Elliot and realized that the friendship would probably not survive these underhanded tactics. Besides, they were too crude for a great mind like his own, Larry thought. He needed something smart and elegant.

Unfortunately, no such idea came to him that morning, so he headed back home for lunch and made plans to head back to his tree that afternoon for some more thinking. On his way back to the tree after lunch, Larry had a bit of an accident. He was thinking so intently about his experiment that he was not paying attention to where he was walking. Larry soon found himself flat on his back.

"That's it!" Larry said to himself. He realized that if he laid a trap for Elliot, he could watch from afar as Elliot tried to get off of his back. Larry was quite pleased with himself, since this plan could conceivably work no matter which member of Elliot's family fell into it. Larry figured that Elliot would probably be suspicious if he found himself on his back so soon after Larry's discussion with him, but Elliot's mom, Peggy, probably wouldn't think anything of it, nor would Elliot's father or twin sisters.

This new idea sent Larry into a sprint to the thinking tree. Now he had something new to think about—how could he come up with a device that would make a turtle fall on its back? Also, how could he accomplish this and make it look like an accident? Larry still had quite a bit to think about.

By the end of the day, Larry was reasonably certain that he had devised a foolproof plan to test out his theory. The next morning, he set out to find all of the materials that he needed to build a device that could flip over a turtle if stepped on. As Larry began assembling the boards and working the mechanism that would flip up when stepped upon, he began to worry about whether this device would hurt anyone. Certainly, most of us would have thought of this very thing to begin with, but as you've already read, Larry doesn't always think of anything other than his immediate plan.

Larry then began to re-evaluate his design. Perhaps the spring wouldn't need to spring up so quickly and a soft bed of leaves could be used to cushion the flipped over turtle's fall. These design changes made Larry fall behind on his contraption, so he cleverly hid it behind his thinking tree that afternoon and made plans to work on it first thing the next morning.

The next day Larry was surprised to see the Owl from the tree walking around the turtle flipper. As Larry approached, the Owl looked up at him. "What is all this, young lemur? You're not planning on building a house here, are you? That's not part of our deal." Larry was surprised, because he had thought that the Owl was vacationing for the week. Otherwise, he wouldn't have decided to build his turtle flipper under the tree for fear of bothering the Owl.

"Oh, that's not a house. I just thought that you were on vacation, so I..."

"You were violating our agreement with a noisy project just because you thought that I was on vacation? You know how much I value my peace and quiet!"

"I'm sorry. I'll take my project elsewhere."

"It's much too late for that, young lemur. You've made me curious. If this isn't some sort of foundation for a secret house, what could it possibly be?"

"Well, it is something I call a *turtle flipper*." Larry looked carefully at the Owl's face to determine what he thought about this idea. The owl looked shocked.

"A turtle flipper? Why would you want to flip a turtle? Did some turtle give you any trouble? If this is the way you treat those who have wronged you in some way, then maybe we should rethink our tree arrangement." Larry's face turned red with embarrassment when he realized how cruel his description of this invention might have sounded.

"Oh, I'm not going to flip a turtle because I'm mad at one. One my best friends is a turtle. I built this device because..." The owl became even more concerned.

"My dear Lemur, I think it would be best if you left this tree and never came back! Imagine, trying to cruelly flip your friend over as a practical joke. Really!"

"No, you've got the wrong idea. This is an experiment!" shouted Larry.

"An experiment? What kind of cruel experiment involves flipping over a helpless turtle? Oh, if this is what you do for fun, I definitely do not want to share this tree with you."

"Well, I just wanted to find out if a turtle could get back on its feet if it was flipped over. My friend Elliot wouldn't let me flip him over to find out and he had never seen another turtle flipped over and..." Larry was interrupted by the owl, who was now chuckling.

"Is that it, then? Well, why didn't you ask me that question?"

"Well," began Larry, who was a bit confused, "You're an owl, and I didn't think you'd know much about turtles."

"Well, you thought wrong, young man. I am an expert on many things, even things from the Lemur world, like Lemurland. My, that place hasn't been the same since they started cutting back on maintenance. I remember when they used to..." The owl began to realize that Larry probably didn't want to hear about maintenance cutbacks and lackluster new ride development and decided to let the little Lemur out of his misery. "Well, in answer to your question, I saw a turtle once who had found himself flipped over onto his back. Needless to say, he tried flipping himself back over and..." The owl paused to add a sense of surprise. This made Larry all the more impatient.

"And...?" asked Larry. The owl was obviously disturbed at Larry's impatience, but decided to let it go.

"I am happy to say that it took that little turtle quite a bit of time, but he soon got back on his feet and began walking away as if nothing had happened."

"Oh. So I guessed right then. I suppose I'll have to find another use for this invention and..."

"I'm not letting you off that easy, young lemur. You need to learn to respect others and not rope them into your experiments without giving them a chance to decide things for themselves." The owl yawned. "Now, if you'll excuse me, I should get on to my nap. Make sure you find a good and decent use for your so-called turtle flipper. I'll see you later." With that, the owl flew back into the deep parts of the tree.

With his question answered, Larry set about figuring out what to do with a turtle flipper. It didn't take long for him to come up with a use for it, however. As he dragged his flipper back home to hide it somewhere in the family's large backyard, he decided just what to do.

So, if you happen to wander into the enchanted Lemur forest and don't scare off any of the animals that live there, you will probably be able to tell which house belongs to Larry's parents. It's the only house with excitable Lemur children flipping around in the backyard on a bizarre contraption that had been originally created to flip over turtles.

While it might seem that things have come to a tidy conclusion, rest assured that there are even more stories to share in the future. After all, with a Lemur like Larry around, there is never a dull moment.

0-595-31815-0

CPSIA information can be obtained at www.ICGtesting.com
Printed in the USA
BVOW08s2158031215

429312BV00001B/40/P